Dear Parents:

Congratulations! Your child is taking the first steps on an exciting journey. The destination? Independent reading!

STEP INTO READING® will help your child get there. The program offers five steps to reading success. Each step includes fun stories and colorful art or photographs. In addition to original fiction and books with favorite characters, there are Step into Reading Non-Fiction Readers, Phonics Readers and Boxed Sets, Sticker Readers, and Comic Readers—a complete literacy program with something to interest every child.

Learning to Read, Step by Step!

Ready to Read   Preschool–Kindergarten
• big type and easy words • rhyme and rhythm • picture clues
For children who know the alphabet and are eager to begin reading.

Reading with Help   Preschool–Grade 1
• basic vocabulary • short sentences • simple stories
For children who recognize familiar words and sound out new words with help.

Reading on Your Own   Grades 1–3
• engaging characters • easy-to-follow plots • popular topics
For children who are ready to read on their own.

Reading Paragraphs   Grades 2–3
• challenging vocabulary • short paragraphs • exciting stories
For newly independent readers who read simple sentences with confidence.

Ready for Chapters   Grades 2–4
• chapters • longer paragraphs • full-color art
For children who want to take the plunge into chapter books but still like colorful pictures.

STEP INTO READING® is designed to give every child a successful reading experience. The grade levels are only guides; children will progress through the steps at their own speed, developing confidence in their reading. The F&P Text Level on the back cover serves as another tool to help you choose the right book for your child.

Remember, a lifetime love of reading starts with a single step!

For our A+ kids, Rory & Tess
—A.S. & R.S.

Text copyright © 2016 by Amy Schmidt
Cover and interior photographs copyright © 2016 by Ron Schmidt
All rights reserved. Published in the United States by Random House Children's Books,
a division of Penguin Random House LLC, New York.

Step into Reading, Random House, and the Random House colophon are registered trademarks
of Penguin Random House LLC.

Visit us on the Web!
StepIntoReading.com
randomhousekids.com

Educators and librarians, for a variety of teaching tools, visit us at
RHTeachersLibrarians.com

Library of Congress Cataloging-in-Publication Data
Names: Schmidt, Amy, author. | Schmidt, Ron, illustrator.
Title: Back to dog-gone school / Amy Schmidt ; illustrated by Ron Schmidt.
Description: New York : Random House Books for Young Readers, 2016. |
Series: Step into reading ; step 2
Identifiers: LCCN 2015029409 | ISBN 978-1-101-93511-8 (softcover) |
ISBN 978-1-101-93512-5 (hardcover) | ISBN 978-1-101-93513-2 (ebook)
Subjects: | BISAC: JUVENILE FICTION / Animals / Dogs. | JUVENILE NONFICTION /
Poetry / Humorous. | JUVENILE FICTION / School & Education.
Classification: LCC PS3619.C4453 A6 2016 | DDC 811/.6—dc23

Printed in the United States of America
10 9 8 7 6 5 4 3 2 1

This book has been officially leveled by using the F&P Text Level Gradient™ Leveling System.

Back to
DOG-GONE
SCHOOL

by Amy Schmidt

photographs by
Ron Schmidt

Random House 🏠 New York

FIRST-DAY JITTERS

I am ready for school.

It is my first day.

I see the bus

heading my way!

Will I like my teacher?

Who will I meet?

Do I have my lunch?

Will I get a seat?

DOG-GONE SCHOOL

Hop on the bus.
No time to wait!

It is time for school.

We cannot be late!

TEACHER'S PET

This is Lucy.

She never makes

the teacher upset.

She can even bark

the alphabet.

Is she helpful?

Oh boy, you bet!

That is why she

is the teacher's pet.

ADD IT UP

Simon lost
two blocks.
Then he lost
two more.
How many blocks
has Simon lost?
The answer
must be four!

SLURP!

Ralphie has
a hallway pass
to visit the
water fountain.
He cannot reach
to get a drink.
So he builds
a book mountain.
Slurp, slurp, slurp.

13

BOYS

With a belly

full of water,

Ralphie sloshes

back to class.

But on his way

he starts to think

he needs a

bathroom pass!

LUNCH BUNCH

We should be eating
lunch right now.
But we just sit
and stare.

Look at
Sammy's cookies!
We hope that
he will share!

D.E.A.R.

Drop

Everything

And

Read!

SPELLBOUND

Maddie has a word

she is working hard

to spell.

Is the letter that

she needs

a B or C or L?

If you know

the missing letter,

go ahead and tell!

HOME FREE

The school bell rings
to end the day.
We all rush out.
It is time to play!

NOT EAT MY HOMEWORK.
NOT EAT MY HOMEWORK.
NOT EAT MY HOMEWORK.
NOT EAT MY HOMEWORK.
NOT EAT MY HOMEWORK.

NOT EAT MY HOMEWORK.
NOT EAT MY HOMEWORK.
NOT EAT MY HOMEWORK.
NOT EAT MY HOMEWORK.
NOT EAT MY HOMEWORK.

NOT EAT MY HOMEWORK.
NOT EAT MY HOMEWORK.
NOT EAT MY HOMEWORK.
NOT EAT MY HOMEWORK.

NOT EAT MY HOMEWORK.
NOT EAT MY HOMEWORK.
NOT EAT MY HOMEWORK.
NOT EAT MY HOMEWORK.

I WILL NOT EAT MY HOMEWORK.
I WILL NOT EAT MY HOMEWORK.
I WILL NOT EAT MY HOMEWORK.
I WILL NOT EAT MY HOMEWORK.
I WILL NOT EAT MY HOMEWORK.
I WILL NOT EAT MY HOMEWORK.
I WILL NOT EAT MY HOMEWORK.
I WILL NOT EAT MY HOMEWORK.
I WILL NOT EAT MY HOMEWORK.
I WILL NOT EAT MY HOMEWORK.
I WILL NOT EAT MY HOMEWORK.
I WILL NOT EAT MY HOMEWORK.
I WILL NOT EAT MY HOMEWORK.
I WILL NOT EAT MY HOMEWORK.
I WILL NOT EAT MY HOMEWORK.
I WILL NOT EAT MY HOMEWORK.
I WILL NOT EAT MY HOMEWORK.
I WILL NOT EAT MY HOMEWORK.

Except for Stan.

He has to stay.

HANGING AROUND

I like to hang around

with my feet above

the ground.

I am missing

just one thing—

a friend to push

this swing!

HOMEWORK

I have my books

at home

to study for a test.

Reading,

spelling,

worksheets.

Will I ever get to rest?

BATH TIME

Playing in mud

makes me feel glad.

I get dirty,

but Mom gets mad.

I take a bath

to wash off the muck.

Has anyone seen

my yellow duck?

BEDTIME

It is time to curl up

in my bed,

to lay down my little

sleepy head.

It is time to dream

the night away

and rest up for

a brand-new day.